Seven Gifts for Cedar

by Cherie Dimaline

Ningwakwe Learning Press
2010

Written by Cherie Dimaline
Illustrated by Grant Nicholson
Layout and Design by Ningwakwe Learning Press

Edited by Mary Shem (B.A./B.Ed./M.Ed)
Reviewed by Talia Morrison, Nancy Cooper, Cathy Shawongonabe and Peter Fergus-Moore

ISBN 978-1-897541-11-1

Library and Archives Canada Cataloguing in Publication

Dimaline, Cherie, 1975-
Seven gifts for cedar / by Cherie Dimaline.

ISBN 978-1-897541-11-1

1. Ojibwa Indians--Juvenile fiction. I. Title.

PS8607.I53S48 2010 jC813'.6 C2010-900641-0

Funding provided by Ontario Ministry of Training, Colleges and Universities.

Printed in Canada 2010
by
Ningwakwe Learning Press
Owen Sound, Ontario
www.ningwakwe.on.ca
1-888-551-9757

Author Cherie Dimaline

Cherie Dimaline is a Métis author from Georgian Bay, Ontario whose work has been featured in national magazines and diverse anthologies. Her first book 'Red Rooms' was published in 2007 and promptly received a Fiction Book of the Year Award. She has since travelled the globe to read at festivals and schools. Cherie is the editor of FNH Magazine, an Aboriginal student publication out of the University of Toronto and has just finished her first full-length novel.

Cherie lives in Toronto with her partner, their three children and two crazy dogs who hog the blankets at night.

"I would like to dedicate this book to
my mother Joanie Dimaline,
whose gifts of unwavering strength and
unconditional love have carried me through."

A "**Families Read Together**" Book

This book has been formatted in a way that encourages parents, extended family members and care-givers to read aloud with young children for the educational and emotional benefits to all involved. When parents embrace their position as their child's most influential role model and understand the value of reading together, the outcomes are positive and measurable.

There are 2 different reading levels in this book. Ontario LBS Reading Level 5, as shown in the smaller-print text, is intended for the adult to read aloud to the child. The larger – print text in the book is intended for the child to read. It is at a grade 2, or LBS Level 2 and the content targets 7-10 year olds.

Through this unique reading format, the parents will be able to contribute to the growth of their children and have a much-needed opportunity to bond with them through a literacy experience.

Table of Contents

Chapter 1
Humility

The year Cedar turned seven, her mother told her that she was old enough to go on a trip all by herself during the summer holidays.

"Yippee!" Cedar yelled as she jumped up from the table with her arms up in the air. She imagined herself holding hands with Mickey Mouse and skipping down a yellow brick road towards the Disney World castle.

Her mother laughed as she watched Cedar dance around the kitchen. Her black pigtails were flying out behind her like windsocks. "I'm glad you're this excited. Auntie Flora will be happy to see you too."

Cedar stopped dancing and her arms fell to her sides. "Auntie Flora?" In her fantasy Mickey Mouse turned into an old lady who wore green rain boots. The path made from yellow bricks changed to a dirt road and the castle became a one-bedroom house with a sagging front porch.

"Yes," her mother said. "Your Great Aunt isn't getting any younger and it would be nice for her to have some company," she explained as she started clearing the dinner plates. "Besides, I'm going to be working all summer and I need someone to keep an eye on you."

Cedar sat down in her chair. She was sad that she was not going to Disney World after all. She was worried that she would be bored at her Auntie's for the whole summer. Then she remembered her favourite cousins who lived nearby and that cheered her up a little.

The next day Cedar's mom helped pack her clothes, toys and books into a red suitcase. They took a taxi to the bus station. Before she got on the bus, Cedar kissed her mom and gave her a big hug. She knew she would miss her a lot.

Flora was really her dad's aunt, which made her Cedar's Great Auntie. When Cedar was little, she thought she was supposed to call her Great because she had done something really good.

Aunt Flora lived on the shores of Georgian Bay, three hours north of the big city. Her house was across the water from the town and beside the reserve where her Dad lived. When Cedar got off the bus, Auntie was there wearing her faded green rain boots under her long skirt in the middle of the summer.

"Ah, my girl," she called loudly and opened her arms wide. Cedar crossed the parking lot and walked into her embrace. She smelled of sweet grass and Ivory soap. "You've gotten so tall," she said.

Cedar's dad was there too! He had come to drive both of them back to Auntie's home. Cedar ran and hugged him really tight. He laughed and said, "I missed you too, kiddo. But wow, it's only been three weeks since I came to visit you at your mom's place."

When she let him go he grabbed the red suitcase from the bus and tossed it into the trunk of his rusty orange sports car. He winked at her over Aunt Flora's shoulder and said, "Welcome home, kid!"

Cedar wrinkled her nose at him. What was that supposed to mean? She didn't live here. She and her mother lived in the city in a cozy apartment way up on the ninth floor.

She sat in the back seat of the car. The wind blew into the open windows and messed up her hair. They drove around the big bay from the town to Auntie's tiny house. Halfway there, the roads became more bumpy and dusty. There were fewer houses and more trees over here than in town. Cedar wondered if there were bears in the trees. She looked into the woods from the car and she watched for scary wild animals.

Auntie held her shiny brown purse tightly on her lap for the whole trip. They pulled into the gravelly driveway and she sprang out of the car like a Pop Tart as soon as they stopped.

ME "I don't like cars, me," she explained. "I'd rather walk than drive any day. That's all we used in the old days, our legs."

Dad handed Cedar her suitcase, tousled her hair and told her, "I'll come back for dinner. Right now I have to go get my friend from Bingo and help her clean her gutters." He jumped back into his car and pulled out onto the road. Dust kicked up from his tires into the still air. Cedar watched him drive away. She struggled to carry her heavy suitcase up to the house, onto the sagging porch and through the squeaky screen door.

Cedar ate lunch with her Auntie. They had toast and jam. Auntie drank tea and Cedar had a glass of milk. Afterwards, they unpacked her red suitcase and put it under the bed.

"I'm going to have a nap," Auntie said.

"Okay," said Cedar. "Can I play outside?"

"Sure," she answered. "Just don't go far and be careful."

"Thank you," Cedar called, running out the front door.

It was warm outside and very, very still. Cedar built little castles in the sand at the end of the driveway and then stomped on them when she grew bored. Not too long later, she heard the sound of children laughing and the crunching of bicycle tires over gravel. Her three cousins Chuck, Cliff and George rode down the road on their hand-me-down bikes, racing each other under the hot sun.

"Hey, you guys!" Cedar said as stood up and waved her arms in the air. "Over here."

One by one, they turned into the driveway and hopped off their bikes, dropping them on the front lawn. "Hey, Cedar," Clifford said, hugging his little cousin. "When did you get here?"

"Just now," she answered, punching Chuck back in the arm in return for his own swing.

George was a little younger and the shyest of the bunch. He kind of hung back from the rest and gave her a little wave when she smiled at him.

"Well, what are you doing? Building apartments for ants or something?" Cliff pointed at her stomped on castles with his lips.

She laughed, "No, I'm just bored is all. What are you guys up to?"

"Just racing," he answered. "Of course I'm winning!"

Chuck pushed his brother. "You wish! Hey, want to come and ride with us? You can double on my bike if you want."

Cedar looked over at the bikes thrown on the lawn. Each one looked as though it had been pieced together out of two or three different bikes. The paint was chipped on one and there were two different sized tires.

"No offense, but I don't think your bikes could handle another person," she laughed. "They look pretty rough."

George kicked at the stones on the ground. Cliff and Chuck looked at their bikes and then at each other, a little embarrassed.

"In the city, I have a new bike. It's red and shiny and goes really fast," she said. "It has ten gears and even has a horn that plays 'Yankee Doodle'. My mom got it for me. It's probably the best bike in the whole world."

The boys walked over to the grass and picked up their bikes. "Uh, well, we should get going. It's getting late," said Cliff.

Cedar was still thinking about her own bicycle. She really wanted to impress her cousins, so she kept on talking. "My mom bought me silver ribbons that hang from the handle grips. I even have a leather seat. Maybe next time, I'll bring it so you can see what a fancy racing bike looks like."

By now her cousins had climbed back onto their own bikes and were peddling towards the road. "Uh, sure, that sounds nice," said Chuck. "See ya!"

"Oh, okay then," Cedar waved. "See you later. Maybe tomorrow?"

"Uh, sure, maybe we'll stop by," yelled Cliff before they disappeared up around the bend.

Cedar looked up to see her Auntie in the window, shaking her permed grey head back and forth. "Why don't you come in for a minute, my girl? I need help putting these dishes away."

Inside, Cedar climbed onto a stepping stool and stacked the small lunch plates onto a shelf over the kitchen sink.

"So, you saw your cousins?" Auntie said.

"Yeah...but just for a minute," Cedar said.

"Oh," said Auntie, sitting at the kitchen table. "Why is that?"

"They had to go," Cedar answered.

"Hmmm, why's that?" Auntie wanted to know.

"They said it was getting late." She put the last plate away and closed the door.

"Hmmm," Auntie looked out the window. "Looks early to me. Could it be that maybe they had to go for another reason?"

Cedar thought about this, climbed off the stool and slid it back into the hall closet. "I don't know."

"Maybe they felt bad about their bikes after a certain girl bragged about her own. Could it be that is the reason why they left in such a hurry?"

Cedar was hurt. “I wasn’t bragging! I just wanted to tell them about my bike because I really like it. That’s all.”

Auntie smiled, “Maybe that’s what you wanted to do, but did you also have to point out what bad shape their bikes were in?”

Cedar thought about it for a minute then tears of shame prickled at the backs of her eyes. “I didn’t mean to make them feel bad. I just wanted them to think I was cool.”

“I know, my girl,” Auntie’s tone softened. She stood up and shuffled to her room to take a nap. “It is important to think about how others may feel before you go talking about how great you are and what kind of stuff you have, even if you think it is really, really great.”

Auntie continued, “It is called Humility and it’s a really important thing to have. Humility does not mean you think less of yourself. It means you think of yourself less.” She patted Cedar on the head and closed her bedroom door behind her.

Cedar thought about it for a minute.

Two days later, Cedar's cousins came by. This time they were walking.

"Hey, Cedar," called Cliff, walking into the backyard where Aunt Flora was showing Cedar how to clean a fish on the picnic table.

"Oh, hi Cliff! Hi guys!" She waved at her other two cousins behind him. "I'm really glad you guys came by."

She felt shy, but really wanted to make things better. "I'm really sorry I bragged about my bike the other day."

Cliff smiled, "Ah, that's okay. I'm sure it is a really nice bike. It's just there are a lot of kids in our family, so sometimes we have to share things like clothes and bikes and they don't always look the best and aren't always new."

"No, I was wrong. I think it's cool that you guys share your stuff and maybe I just felt shy 'cause I'm not from here. So I bragged a little. I'm sorry if I made you feel bad."

"Hey, Cedar," Chuck said, walking forward to punch her in the arm again. "Just 'cause you live in the city with your mom doesn't mean 'you're not from here.' You're family even if you are a whiney girl." He laughed as he dodged her return punch.

"Yeah, so let's say we all go down to the shore and swim. Is that okay, Auntie?" Cliff asked his Great Aunt who was sitting at the table with freshly cut trout fillets in front of her.

"Oh sure. You kids go and have a good time." Auntie said.

They ran off together in the direction of the house and grabbed towels and snacks. Cedar stopped near the door, turned back to run to her Auntie and hugged the old woman from behind, "Miigwetch, Auntie." Then she ran off to join her cousins.

Chapter 2
WISDOM

YOU

The next few weeks went by quickly. The days were packed, full of swimming, tree-climbing, fishing with her Dad after work and staying up late listening to Great Auntie Flora snoring in her flowered kerchief.

One Sunday when it was really hot outside, Cedar and Auntie spent the morning cleaning scraps from the yard. They were both tired, but especially Auntie who went to her bedroom to take a nap when they were done. Cedar sat on the scratchy brown couch. Her dad was still at work down at the marina so she couldn't play with him yet. She turned on the tiny TV in the living room to find cartoons but there were only two channels and they were both news channels. She turned it off and went outside.

Cedar made a tent under the picnic table with some old blankets and some clothes pins. She pretended she was a pirate in a little dark boat. The grass was the wide sea. She peeked out from a hole between the clothes pins and looked for sharks or her favourite cousins. Neither of them showed up.

Eventually, Cedar got bored and wandered back inside just as Great Aunt Flora was coming out of her bedroom. Her curly hair was tucked loosely under a bright blue kerchief.

"Hey, kwe-zaanz, my girl," she called just as Cedar was getting ready to flop back onto the old couch. "Are you too busy to come on a walk with your old Auntie, then?"

Cedar's face brightened up immediately. She remembered what her mom once said about how Auntie was interesting and still very active in her age. "Sure, Auntie, I would love to come with you," she said as she pulled her shoes back on and headed out the door onto the sun-baked porch.

"Where are we going anyways?" she asked.

Auntie laughed and said, "Hee hee. You should always know what it is you're agreeing to before you agree to something."

Cedar was worried now. "Well, I just trust you, I guess."

Auntie grabbed and held her great niece's hand. "I trust you too."

They swung their hands in a big arc. Auntie answered, "I'm going to take you to pick medicine."

This sounded odd to Cedar who got her medicine at the pharmacy with her mother. She pictured herself and Auntie toiling in the hot summer sun, bent over capsule bushes, picking brightly coloured pills and putting them in little round containers clipped onto a wide leather belt.

It was such a strange idea that she was quiet for the whole walk. They walked down the winding pathway behind the house, then along the shoreline and into a small field half hidden by draping willow trees. When they finally stopped she was surprised at her wild surroundings.

Everything was green. Tall trees surrounded them and long grass was under their feet. The spaces in between the trees were filled with bushes, and vines snaked up the tree trunks. Cedar was scared only for a minute when Auntie let go of her hand.

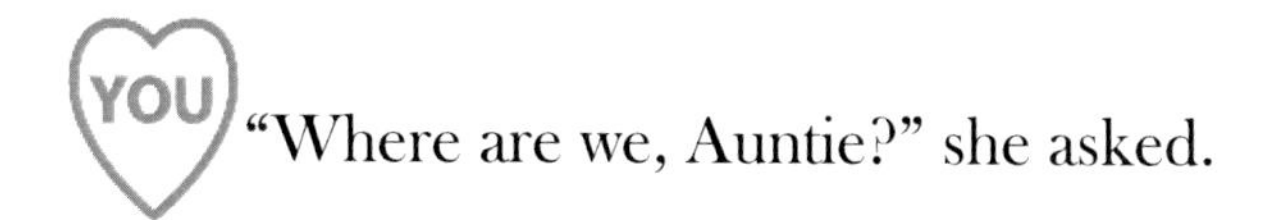

"Where are we, Auntie?" she asked.

"In the bush," Auntie answered as she pulled dry, brown leaves out of her apron pocket. Cedar heard her talk in a language she sometimes heard her mom use when she talked on the phone to someone from back home. Then she put some of the dry leaves on the ground and picked up a green plant and put it in a cloth bag she had brought with her. Right away the air was filled with a sweet, spicy smell that made Cedar feel safe.

"What's that, Auntie?" she couldn't help asking.

"This, my girl," said Auntie, pointing to another plant just like the first one, "is Sage. This is medicine."

"What's that brown stuff you're putting on the ground?"

"That is sayma, tobacco. It is also medicine. We leave it as an offering of thanks for the plants that we take from the earth. It's called doing things in a good proper way."

Cedar watched her old Auntie as she prayed and picked. Aunt Flora never forgot to put down an offering even for the smallest plant. Cedar felt proud and more grown up for having gone on this important trip. After a while when Auntie was done, she said one last prayer and turned to leave.

"Wait, Auntie," Cedar called, running over to a corner of the clearing. "There are lots and lots of plants over here."

"That's okay," Auntie called back, "I only take what I need." She held up her cloth bag. "And this is all I need right now."

Cedar hesitated, thinking about how when there was a sale on something at the grocery store, she and her mom often grabbed as much as they could carry home. She figured out then that this wasn't the same thing.

She ran to catch up to Auntie. This time she grabbed the older woman's hand first as they tromped through the bush together.

"Auntie, I like how you teach me things when I'm here."

The old woman smiled. "Learning is important. Don't your teachers tell you that?"

"Yeah, but this is different," Cedar struggled to say what she meant. "It's like I learn things in school because I have to. I say them over and over again so they stick in my head. The stuff you teach me just kind of grows there and it gets bigger and bigger on its own. Like one of those plants."

Auntie squeezed Cedar's little fingers in between her own thick, calloused fingers. "You're not just getting knowledge. You are getting wise. That is Wisdom."

Cedar was about to ask what that meant. She paused for a minute and thought about it and after she knew exactly what it meant. It was the difference between just grabbing groceries off a shelf or going for a walk in the woods and learning to search for the plant that you know will help your body.

She vowed to spend a lot more time with her wise Auntie that summer.

CHAPTER 3
RESPECT

At the end of the summer, Cedar's Dad took her for a relaxing 'Daddy-Daughter' drive around the bay. They listened to Dad's country music very loud and sang the parts they knew at the top of their lungs.

When they got back to Auntie's house, Clifford, Chuck and George were waiting out by the front of the house for her. Their bikes were sprawled across the lawn and Auntie Flora was sitting in a folding chair on the little porch.

"Hey, cuz!" Clifford waved. "Good to see you!"

"Yeah, took ya long enough to get here," Chuck smirked at Cedar's Dad. "Driving like an old lady again, I suppose?"

He chased his little nephew around the yard while George pointed and laughed.

"Oh you think that's funny, do you?" Dad swooped down and scooped George up onto his shoulders and he carried him along in the chase.

Auntie laughed, "Oh, you kids. I'm going in to make some tea and rest for a bit." She climbed the steps and went inside the cool, dark house.

After Dad left, the four cousins decided to head down to the shore and get some swimming in before supper. Cedar ran inside and quickly changed into her bathing suit. She grabbed some towels out of the linen closet.

"Hey, Cedar," Chuck called in the open window. "Grab some snacks too, eh?"

Cedar looked into the cupboards. She took out peanut butter and jam. Then she got the bread from the counter and made four sandwiches. She wrapped each of them in plastic wrap and put all four into a plastic bag. Then she took four juice boxes from the fridge and put them into the bag too.

She carried the towels and their snacks outside and they all marched down the hill to the shore. The hill was steep in some places so they had to be careful and hold onto branches in some areas. When they got to the bottom, they threw their stuff on the picnic table. They walked straight down across from the dock and jumped, one by one, into the lake.

The water was cold. It almost hurt to jump into it, but after the first minute, it felt really great. Cedar and her cousins bobbed to the surface laughing. Little George jumped in and out of the water around them like a shiny brown fish. Chuck chased after him and Clifford started a splash war with Cedar. They were the only ones there and it was as if they had their own private beach. They felt like millionaires.

After an hour of playing, the millionaires sat on the dock with their feet dangling off the side, eating peanut butter sandwiches in the sunshine. It felt good to be there and great to be with her family. This really was starting to feel like home for her.

Lunch time ended when Chuck pushed George off the dock.

SPLASH!

George popped up just under his brother's feet and pulled him in. The crust from Chuck's sandwich floated under the dock.

ME

After swimming for a few hours, the cousins decided to call it a day. They carried their damp towels over their shoulders and trudged back up the hill. At the top, Cedar turned back to look at the peaceful bay.

She noticed the plastic bag that they had carried their sandwiches in was still sitting out at the end of the dock. She was about to run and get it, but her cousins were already half way up the hill. She decided to leave it and ran to catch up to them.

She promised herself she would pick it up tomorrow.

The next morning Auntie shook her awake. Cedar was reluctant to open her eyes and when she did, she saw that the sun had barely risen. The room was still dark. She rolled over on the narrow cot.

"What time is it Auntie?"

"Morning," was the answer. "Get up! We need to go for a walk."

Cedar rolled out of bed. She put her jeans on and a t-shirt she had thrown onto the floor the day before. Yawning, she followed the old lady out the front door and around the house.

Auntie led her down the hill to the shore. Cedar had to hurry to keep up.

"Is everything okay?" Cedar asked.

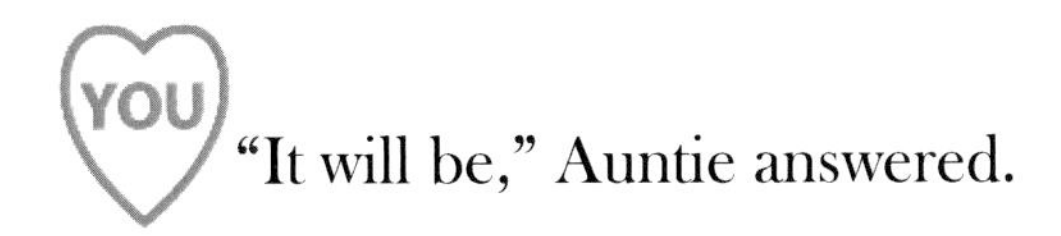

"It will be," Auntie answered.

Aunt Flora led her to the edge of the water. Her sandals were getting wet with the ripples that crept up the sandy shore. There, at her feet, was a dark green turtle, it was the size of a dinner plate. Cedar ran beside her Auntie. She was excited to see a real live turtle this close. She had only seen one behind the glass at the pet store.

"COOL," she said. She watched it for a minute as it pulled its head into its crusty shell. Its eyes rolled back and forth, warily watching the humans. Puzzled, she turned to her Auntie. "But why isn't it running away? I thought turtles were shy of people?"

"They are," Auntie answered. "And I'm sure it would be well on his way, if it wasn't for this." Auntie bent down and carefully flipped the turtle onto his back. There, wrapped around three of its legs and tangled up under its shell, was a white plastic grocery bag.

Cedar gasped, "Oh no! Is it going to be okay?"

"Yes, I suppose it will be after we cut it loose," Auntie answered as she carried it up to the picnic table.

"How could this happen?" Cedar asked, feeling her anger rising. She was angry at the careless people who polluted the lake and hurt little turtles.

"I don't know. Someone must have left this down by the water and this turtle found it along its travels."

Auntie gently pulled the bag from one of the openings in the turtle's shell where it had been partially pushed. The grocery store logo became clear and Cedar was sure she could smell the strong scent of peanut butter.

Cedar gasped. She swung around to look at the dock. It was empty. It suddenly dawned on her that this bag was hers, that she was the careless person who was hurting little turtles. She felt tears burning the backs of her eyes.

She began to sob. Aunt Flora looked up at her. “Are you okay, kwe-zaanz?”

“Auntie, that bag is mine. I brought it down here yesterday when we were swimming. I left it on the dock.” One fat tear rolled down her cheek and landed on the picnic table beside the upturned turtle.

Auntie smiled gently and Cedar knew that the old woman already knew it belonged to her.

“I was going to pick it up today,” she sobbed again, another tear running down her cheek. “But it musta blown into the water.”

Auntie carefully cut the bag away with a green-handled paring knife she carried in her apron pocket. “Well, my girl, sometimes we have to learn lessons the hard way. Do you know what this lesson is?” She waited a moment then looked up at her great niece with kindness in her old eyes, “It’s Respect, kwe-zaanz.”

Cedar thought about it. She knew that she would never be lazy with her responsibilities again. She knew that she would consider other creatures beside herself and that she would work hard to make sure her actions didn’t affect others in a negative way. She was still thinking when Auntie cut the last piece of plastic free.

“It’s really important to take care of the earth and all those that live on it,” Auntie said as she walked down to the water. The turtle was balanced carefully on her flat palms. “We are all part of a circle; all connected in one way or the other. When one of us gets hurt or neglected, we all feel it.”

She placed the turtle on the sandy shore and slowly backed away and stood beside her great niece. After a moment, the turtle extended its legs and its head. It looked around, and then pushed itself into the lake, drifting away like a lost Frisbee on the surface.

ME

"Respect," Cedar said as she watched the turtle make its way through the hanging willow branches that dipped into the lake like long, skinny fingers. "I'll always have respect."

Auntie chuckled, putting her arm around the little girl. The sun had climbed over the edge of the bay, throwing light onto the water like a thousand shiny dimes thrown across the surface. "You're already half way there."

CHAPTER 4
BRAVERY

The next summer, Cedar and her red suitcase arrived in her dad's car at Great Aunt Flora's house just after lunch hour. Now that she was eight years old and a lot taller, she had less trouble hauling her own luggage. Aunt Flora didn't make it into town to pick her up at the station this year.

Cedar wasn't really surprised, as her mother had already explained to her that she should be prepared to help out a little more on her trips.

"Your Auntie is getting older," her mother said. She was sitting on the bed watching her daughter pack.

"I know," Cedar answered.

"So I would be very proud of you if you helped her as much as you can," she said.

"I will, mom," she answered. "I love Auntie. I will try to do as much as I can."

"That's my girl," her mother said.

She was happy to be here with her dad again. He drove her across the bay, filling her in on all the stories since the last time he had visited her in the city. Soon, they pulled up in front of Auntie's house with the sloping porch.

"Okay sweetie, I'll be back for dinner," he said and leaned over and kissed her on the forehead.

"Okay, dad, see you then," she said as she jumped out of the car.

Now inside the house, Cedar quietly placed her suitcase beside the kitchen table and slipped back out the screen door. Soft snores sounded from the bedroom. She looked around for something to do outside until Auntie's nap time was over. The yard was messy with weeds and the garden was completely overgrown with them. She went to the back shed and got a small spade and started digging the weeds out by their roots. She hummed as she worked and the time went by quickly.

The bang of the screen door pulled Cedar out of her day dream. She was still on her hands and knees spreading the soil in the garden with smooth, looping swirls of her shovel. She looked over her shoulder and saw Aunt Flora on the front porch smiling down at her.

"Ah, my girl, you're here," she said as she carefully made her way down the stairs. "Boy did I miss you," she added.

She stopped when she got to the bottom of the stairs. "What's this? Oh my, my yard looks great! Chi miigwetch!" She looked around her property with a big smile on her old face and walked to the garden to hug Cedar. "What a nice girl you are!"

"Hey, Jones!" came a yell from the road. It was Cliff, Chuck and George. Little Georgie hit quite a growth spurt over the past year because he was nearly as tall as Chuck now, yet he was still just as quiet as ever. "Wanna come for a ride?" Cliff asked.

Last summer Auntie had picked up an older bike from a cousin up the road and it was in the back shed. She was tempted. Instead, Cedar waved and called back, "I'm going to put my stuff away first and have some tea, maybe I'll catch up in a bit."

"Okay, suit yourself," Chuck called back. "We'll be over by the baseball diamond."

Cedar put the shovel back in the shed and went to have tea with her Auntie. She noticed that the old lady moved more slowly this year. It took a lot longer for her to get around the house. When she carried the full kettle to the stove, her arm shook.

After they had tea and some scone, Cedar helped clean up the dishes. "Auntie, is it okay if I go play with the guys?"

"Oh yes, go play, my girl," she answered. "I'm fine, me."

ME

“Thank you!” she yelled, running out the door and around the back to get her bike. She pulled the old ten-speed out, rode it down the gravel driveway and onto the side of the road. It was wobbly for a while but she got used to it.

It was a lot bigger than her city bike but after a few minutes, she was sailing along, the wind blowing her hair back over her shoulders.

She turned off onto the grassy field towards the baseball diamond. At first she thought her cousins were huddled by the home plate because they were standing in a circle. She rode through the outfield and over the pitcher’s mound, slowing down as she got closer.

She got off the bike and leaned it up against the batting cage since it didn’t have a kickstand. Then she walked over to home plate. Her three cousins were standing in a circle and in the middle was a short, chubby boy named Roger. He was actually related to them all in some distant way, like a second cousin.

She heard Chuck speak first. “Well, are you going to prove that you can do it or what?”

“Yeah, Roger, show us all how you’re better than us,” said Cliff.

Roger looked scared as he was surrounded by the taller boys.

"STOP IT!"

His expression gave Cedar a queasy feeling in her stomach. He gave a nervous giggle. “Come on you guys, I… I’m not wearing the right shoes to do it. How about …um, some other day?”

“No way,” Cliff said. “How about right now? Unless you can’t do it.”

“Do what?” Cedar asked. Up until now no one noticed that she was there.

“Hey, Jones! Roger here was making fun of George because he couldn’t make it to the top of the cage. He says that he can climb up one side and down the other in under 5 minutes. So we want to see it, and now he’s being a baby.”

“Am not!” Roger shrieked, squaring his shoulders. When the boys glared at him he quickly reverted to his slouched stance.

“Are too!” Cliff roared. “And now we’re not leaving until Roger here does what he says he can do. We want to see him climb the whole cage in less than 5 minutes.” He pushed Roger in the chest making the smaller boy stumble and his face crumple up in fear.

“I’m sorry,” Roger mumbled.

“What’s that, I don’t think I caught that?” Chuck asked, cupping his hand around his ear.

“I said I’m sorry.” Roger mumbled again.

“Sorry for what?” Chuck asked.

“Sorry for making fun of George. And sorry for bragging,” he answered, kicking at the dirt with his running shoes.

“I’m not sure that’s enough,” Cliff said. “I think you have to go ahead and prove yourself Roger, my good man.”

The smaller boy shook his head, eyes wide with fear. “Please don’t.”

The three boys started moving Roger towards the back of the fence. “Yeah,” George said. “Show us, you big show off!”

ME

"No! Really, I can't. Don't make me," Roger yelled.

"STOP IT!" The scream made everyone stop. For a second, even Cedar didn't move until she realized that it was her yell.

Clifford turned to her. "What's your problem?"

Cedar herself felt bullied by her older cousin now as he walked towards her. Normally a happy boy, Cliff seemed to have taken on a different personality this afternoon. He seemed like a bully to her and she felt her knees go weak as he approached.

Cedar looked over at Roger. Tears welled up in his big brown eyes as he watched her with a mixture of desperation and hope. So instead of running, she stood her ground, dug in her heels and lifted her chin.

"Stop being such a bully, Clifford. He said he was sorry and you need to respect that."

She looked around at the other three boys. She felt like her mother just now. "You too, Chuck. And you, Georgie, I'm surprised with you. You know better than that."

She said exactly what her mother said to her when she got in trouble. George looked down, suddenly finding something very interesting with his red and blue tennis shoes.

She looked at Roger his eyes were drying up now. "And Roger, don't make fun of people." She thought she should say something else. She bit her lip and thought about what else her mother would say right now. "Mmm, oh, and next time you should think before you talk." She finished by shaking her finger in his face. There, now she was a real grown up.

She sighed deeply and gave all the boys her meanest stare. Then she walked to her bike and lifted it off the fence. She was just about to hop on and ride back to her Auntie's when she heard Roger speak.

"Hey, Cedar, aren't you going to stay and play baseball with us?"

It was as if nothing happened and everything was back to normal. Chuck and George threw the scuffed up baseball to each other. Roger was jogging to the pitcher's mound and Cliff had picked up the bat.

She didn't know if she'd ever understand boys, but she put her bike down and ran to man first base anyways.

That night after supper, Cedar explained the whole scene to Aunt Flora.

"Hmm, sounds like you had an interesting afternoon," Auntie said.

"Yeah, it was kind of scary too," Cedar answered.

"How's that my girl? You don't think your cousins would hurt you do you?" Auntie, asked.

"No, not at all," Cedar answered. "But, it was kind of scary standing up to a group of people, I guess. It was weird being the only one who felt different."

"I see," Auntie answered, taking a sip from her cup of tea. "I understand what it is you're saying. It takes Bravery to stand up and be heard, especially when you're the only one saying it."

Cedar thought about it for a minute, "Yeah, that's what it was like but I don't really think I was that brave."

"Oh yes, my girl! Bravery is another important teaching, and today you learned that all by yourself." She reached across the table and lifted Cedar's chin so that they were looking directly into each other's eyes.

"It is a big lesson, sometimes a scary lesson, and you have learned it. I am proud of you."

Cedar got a different kind of feeling in her stomach from the one she had today at the baseball diamond. It made her want to sit very straight and smile, and that is exactly what she did.

Chapter 5
HONESTY

YOU

One afternoon, about three weeks after the incident at the baseball diamond, Cedar sat in the sun reading a book. She brought it from home. It was about a wizard that went to a big school with all kinds of other wizards and witches. It was her favourite and she was almost done.

When she finished the very last page, she put it down and went into the house to get a drink of juice. She saw red Kool-Aid in a plastic container when she opened the fridge. "Yum!" She said to herself as she carried it over to the counter and put it down.

Cedar reached up as high as she could to get a glass down from the cupboard. She could barely reach the second shelf. She really had to stretch and lean over to get it. Her fingers closed around a plastic tumbler at the very same second that she bumped the half full container of red juice and knocked it over.

SPLASH!

In a great red wave, the entire contents poured out onto the counter, spilled onto the tiled floor and all down Cedar's front. She pulled her hands down and jumped back but it was too late. It was horrible. The entire counter was covered with Kool-Aid and the floor was stained with red splashes.

"Oh no!" Cedar didn't know what to do. "This is the worst day ever! This couldn't be any worse."

Just then the tumbler she had been pulling to the edge of the shelf fell from the cupboard and hit her on the head.

"Great!" she said, rubbing her head.

And then it got even worse. On the counter she saw a big, yellow envelope with her Auntie's name written on the back in careful cursive writing, except that now the ink had started to smear and it was drenched in Kool-Aid. It floated down the counter like a flat boat on a sugary sea. Cedar snatched up the envelope and ran outside to put it in the sun to dry while she cleaned up the mess.

She started drying with paper towels to soak up the counter puddle. When that was done, she grabbed the mop out of the hall closet and got the floor cleaned. She soaped up a rag with really hot water and carefully cleaned up every trace of the red sticky stuff. Then she washed the juice container and the tumbler in the sink, dried them and put everything away. No one would ever know how bad the mess had been if they walked in now. She felt better in the clean kitchen. She felt a lot better when she thought of how fast she cleaned the kitchen until she remembered the yellow envelope on the porch.

Throwing the mop back in the closet on the way out, Cedar headed out onto the porch. The envelope was on the stair railing; its edges had curled up in the sun. The sun had done a good job of drying it out and now only the very middle was still damp. Unfortunately, it had also seemed to bake in the dye from the Kool-Aid. The whole thing was a sickly pink colour now.

"Oh no!"Cedar moaned as she picked up the crispy paper. "It's totally ruined."

Then she had a horrifying thought. What if what was inside was really important! She pried open the glue that held the flap down and reached inside. She grabbed a few pieces of thick paper and pulled them free from the sticky insides of the envelope. Everything smelled like cherry flavoured juice.

In her hand were two really old photographs. They had been black and white, but now they were black and white, and pink. In the first picture, a little boy of about three years old sat on the back of a spotted pony. He had two crooked front teeth and wore pants that were too short in the legs. The second picture, which was kind of stuck to the first one, was of a man and a woman posing together in front of an old white clapboard house. They were both smiling with big huge smiles stretched across their wrinkled brown faces, like someone had just told a good joke. The man wore suspenders and a button-down shirt. The woman wore a flowered dress with a high collar.

ME

It was worse than she thought. These pictures looked important and one-of-a-kind. Suddenly she heard her Auntie get out of bed. The old box spring mattress squeaked and creaked as she sat up.

Cedar heard the bathroom door shut and panicked. Any minute now Auntie would come out to the kitchen and see the terrible mess she had made of these keepsakes. In her panic, Cedar decided to shove the pictures back into the envelope and stashed them under the stairs of the porch.

She had been sitting back in her chair on the porch, holding her finished book open as if she had been reading this whole time when Aunt Flora came outside.

"There you are, my girl," Aunt Flora smiled when she saw Cedar sitting in the chair, pretending to read.

Cedar put her book down, "Oh, hi Auntie." She stood and kissed the old woman on her soft cheek. "I was just reading."

"Well then, come in and we'll have a snack." She said as she turned and went back inside. Stealing a glance at the front stairs, Cedar followed her in. She felt light headed and was so nervous her hands were shaking.

Auntie had her head in the fridge. "Hmmm, did you see a jug of juice in here?"

Cedar felt like she might throw up. "Oh, yeah...I was really thirsty when I got back from bike riding and I drank it all."

"Oh, okay," the old lady smiled and took out milk instead. "That's okay, it was for you anyways." Very slowly, Auntie got down two glasses and filled them half way, one for each of them. Then she took out some soft oatmeal cookies from the breadbox and carried them to the table as well. She was just about to sit down when she remembered something. "Oh, I almost forgot..."

She struggled to stand straight and turned to the counter. She looked all over the counter and for a very long minute, Cedar was sure she was busted. She was sure her Auntie could smell the cleaner she used or maybe she saw that she missed a spot cleaning.

"I was sure I put it here," she said as she felt around the counter, as if she didn't trust her eyes and needed to feel around to make sure. "I put an envelope here just this morning."

Cedar's eyes got bigger and she made herself busy by tearing one of the cookies apart and stuffing it into her mouth. Her nerves made it almost impossible to swallow the food and she had to wash it down with big gulps of cold milk.

"Cedar," Auntie asked, "Did you see a yellow envelope here?"

"No!" Cedar answered. It hurt her head to lie, but she felt like she had to.

"That's too bad," Auntie answered. She turned around and sat down at the table. But she didn't eat. She didn't even drink her milk. She just looked confused. "It bugs me that I can't remember things."

Cedar felt bad. She didn't want her Auntie to feel like this was because she couldn't remember things. But she couldn't tell her the truth that she had ruined the envelope and the pictures inside. And now that she had already lied, it was too late. If she told her the truth now, Auntie would think Cedar was a liar.

"I asked your Uncle Randy to take some old photos of your dad and your grandparents into town yesterday and to get them blown up so you could take them home with you. I wonder what happened to them."

ME

Auntie looked so worried and so confused that Cedar burst into tears.

She put her head down on the table and cried. Her cookie fell into little pieces in front of her.

"Oh my! What's wrong, dear?" her Great Aunt said with concern.

"Auntie, I ruined the pictures," she sobbed. "I spilled the juice and the pictures got all wrecked."

"What?" Aunt Flora was surprised at the confession. "What do you mean ruined? Are they in the garbage?"

"No," Cedar sniffed, "I hid them under the front porch." She lifted her head slightly and pointed to the screen door.

She couldn't be sure, but Cedar thought she heard her Auntie chuckle.

"That's exactly where your father used to hide things" she said.

Cedar continued, "And now I lied to you." She broke out into fresh tears.

"Why don't you settle down and fetch the pictures?" Aunt Flora said.

Cedar got up from the table and wiped the salty tears off her cheeks with the back of her hand. "Okay."

She went outside and bent over the edge of the porch to reach underneath the hollow stairs and grabbed the envelope. She brushed off a spider and carried the envelope back inside the house.

"Now, let's have a look here," Auntie said softly. She pulled out the two photos, one by one. They were curled now around the edges of the envelope and still stained of bright pink in all the spots that were supposed to be white.

She held out the picture of the little boy on the pony. "Well, doesn't your dad look handsome with such rosy cheeks?"

Reluctantly, Cedar looked up at the picture being held out. She saw what appeared to be blush applied to Dad's cheeks. She giggled a bit, but when she noticed that his eyes were red like a demon, she broke out in peals of laughter.

"Dad looks evil," she laughed. Auntie looked at the picture again and joined in the laughter.

When they calmed down, Auntie took both of Cedar's hands into her own and held them across the wooden table. "My girl, nothing can ever be so bad that you have to hide the truth. Don't you feel better now that I know what really happened?"

Cedar checked. Her chest didn't feel tight and her light-headedness was gone. She nodded. "I'm sorry, Auntie."

"That's okay. These were copies of pictures I already have. We'll just ask Randy to make another trip into town. But more important than any pictures is being honest. Honesty is another lesson that one must learn to live Pimaatisiwin."

"What's that, Auntie?"

"Pimaatisiwin? That means the Good Life, my girl. It is what you live by when you follow the Seven Grandfather Teachings. Those are the teachings handed down by the first Anishinaabe Grandfathers as instructions. If we're lucky, we learn them early on so we can live in a good way."

Cedar sniffed again and thought for a minute. "So I'm lucky then that I spilled Kool-Aid all over the kitchen?"

Auntie laughed, "Yes my girl, and so am I." She looked around the room, her arms open, "Now I don't have to wash the floor like I was going to tomorrow!"

CHAPTER 6
TRUTH

ME

Cedar read a lot that summer. One of the books she really loved was a picture book with fancy diagrams. It was a book about the human body.

She thought maybe she would be a doctor one day. She wasn't quite sure about the body and the way it worked but it was all really interesting to her. She took out books from the library about the body, like bones and the five senses.

Time went by quickly for Cedar. She spent a lot of time listening to her Auntie who was in a storytelling mood that summer.

When they weren't picking berries, plants and firewood, she and Auntie were baking scone, making soup or playing cards. Cedar also spent the days biking with her cousins, fishing at the spots Auntie had showed them and yielded the best catch. She was just generally enjoying summer on the bay. Before she knew it, August was drawing to a close.

The day before she was supposed to leave Cedar went on a long bike ride with the guys. They raced to the baseball diamond, took a break to skip rocks at the beach and tested their bravery by jumping over fallen branches by the big woods.

Just before it was time to turn back for supper, they saw a group of the older kids by Joanie's store. One of them called out, "Hey, Cliff," and waved him over.

Clifford went first and the rest of them followed him across the parking lot in a line. There were three boys and two girls. Cedar thought they all looked grumpy, like they had just gotten out of bed or something. She noticed that a lot of older kids looked like this, as though they had to put on a mean face on purpose.

"Babysitting?" the boy who seemed to be the leader asked. The two girls giggled. Cliff turned red.

"No, just taking my cousin for a ride before she heads back to the city," he pointed at Cedar with his chin.

They all looked at Cedar. She held her head straight and tried to copy their hard looks right back at them.

"Hey, kid!" the boy said and then asked her, "How old are you?"

She tried to sound cool, "I'll be nine soon."

They all laughed. One of the girls said, "I remember nine. Oh the carefree days of childhood." They laughed again. They must have been eleven at the most.

"I'm not a child," Cedar said daringly. She narrowed her eyes and spit into the dust beside her feet. Spitting was gross, but she saw how the bad guys did it in the movies, so she figured it would make her look tougher.

"Yeah, yeah," the boy dismissed her, turning back to her older cousin. "Hey, Cliff, check out the new jump we just made, my man."

He pointed underneath one of the other boys. "Jared, get your butt off there!"

Jared stood up quickly. "Sorry, Trav."

"What's that? Chuck asked his face twisted in confusion at the pile of broken boards and rusty nails that sat there.

JOANIE'S

ME

“What’s that!” Travis repeated. “What that is, is the most feared bike jump in Tiny Township?”

“We made it ourselves and we’re gonna take our bikes off it. I figure we could catch some real air time off this puppy.” He was still pointing at the homemade dangerous contraption.

He turned to the newcomers, pointing his finger at each of their faces with a challenging smirk, “Want a ride? Or are you too widdle?” The girls giggled again.

Cliff frowned, “I’m no baby, Travis.” He moved his bike beside the big kids so that now he was facing Cedar and his brothers from the opposite side of the circle. George and Chuck silently shook their heads and started backing away from the group, pushing their bikes back towards the road.

Now it was Cedar’s turn. Travis turned to look her straight in the face and his mean blue eyes squinted up into what he figured was a menacing look.

She thought about it for a minute, looking over the boy’s shoulder at the mess of splinters and rust. She imagined sitting at the doctor’s office while he dug huge needles of wood out of her behind. In her imagination, she looked like a huge porcupine with wooden spikes popping out of her rear.

She could almost feel the sting of the nurse’s iodine.

While she thought of how badly she could get hurt and imagined the insides of her body sticking out of the outsides, like a sock pulled off real fast, the older kids moved the bike jump to the middle of the parking lot.

She looked up and saw that the kids were all on their bikes now, circling around the jump like a swarm of bees in denim shorts. Chuck and George were over by the road but Cliff was on his bike with his feet planted on the ground, positioned right in front of the ramp.

"Jump! Jump! Jump!" All the kids chanted in unison.

Travis watched the fear in Cedar's eyes when she saw her cousin getting ready to do something really dangerous. "Ha, guess not everyone in this family is a chicken." Then he picked up his bike and joined the circle, adding his voice to the yell, "JUMP! JUMP! JUMP!"

Cedar couldn't stay there. She had to do something. If not, Clifford could get really hurt. She didn't care if they called her a chicken. She didn't care if they thought she was a little kid. She had to follow her instincts and do what she knew was right.

"JUMP! JUMP! JUMP!" They all screamed it now, circling faster and faster. Cedar's heart was beating really hard. She saw sweat on Cliff's forehead and knew that he must be scared.

Then Cedar saw her chance. One of the boys, a short guy with smaller legs, was a little slower than the rest of them and there was a space in the circle for her to ride between him and the spiky haired girl who rode in front of him. Cedar watched them and her cousin go around the ramp once more before she made her move. Just as Clifford put his feet on the pedals, gave a push and his bike started forward towards the ramp, Cedar knew sure injury was going to occur. She sprang into action.

"NOOOOO!" She yelled as she pedaled as fast as she could. She pedaled so fast that she made it through the gap between the short bully and the spiky haired girl and rode into the middle ground. She rode her bike across the lot and in between her cousin and the broken down ramp, so that he had to slam on his brakes to avoid crashing into her. She closed her eyes as he got closer. She could hear his brakes on the pavement.

And then there was nothing. No crash. No squealing tires. Nothing. She opened her eyes. Clifford had stopped just in time. His shocked face was inches from hers. He was so close that she could smell his bologna breath.

Travis threw down his bike in disgust. “Ha, I knew it! You’re still a baby,” he laughed. One of the girls laughed with him while the other looked green, like she was going to throw up from witnessing a near collision.

Cedar smirked at him while climbing back onto her bike. “If being smart enough to not hurt myself or let my cousin kill himself is being a baby, then, I don’t want to grow up.”

Just then there was a loud ‘crack’ and the groan of wood. They turned just in time to see the ramp fall into a million broken pieces. There was a big cloud of dust and then nothing, just a pile of scrap wood. No one said a word.

Cedar rode away from the older kids. She was not sure if Cliff was even with her until she felt his hand on her back. She turned around and saw him riding close to her side. She smiled back at him, and yelled, “Race you to the field!”

And off they sped.

That night while they were playing ‘Go Fish’ at the kitchen table, Cedar told her Auntie everything that had happened that day, including how she almost considered taking the jump because she felt pressured.

“But you didn’t take it,” Auntie said, putting down a pair of sixes. “Why not?”

“Well, because I thought it was stupid to do something just because somebody else wanted you to. Especially when you knew it wasn’t the right thing to do.”

“And why is that, my girl?”

“Because I think it’s more important to be who you are and to make decisions for yourself. I don’t want to hurt myself or anyone else just to be cool or fit in,” she answered.

"That is called Truth, and it is another teaching on the way to Pimaatisiwin," Auntie said, smiling at Cedar.

Cedar was confused, "Isn't being truthful just being honest?"

"Kind of.... It's being honest and living true to yourself and your family. It's living with honour and integrity, and the choice you made today was a very honourable one." Then she put down the last cards in her hand and laughed. "I win!"

CHAPTER 7
LOVE

ME The next summer, when Cedar was nine, she came home from the last day of school to find her red suitcase packed and sitting by the front door. She was surprised to see a larger blue suitcase decorated with big yellow daisies beside it.

"Mom?" she called into the kitchen. "Why are there two suitcases here? Did you pack me extra stuff?"

"Kind of. I packed you an extra parent," she said over her shoulder while making cucumber sandwiches at the counter.

"Huh?" Cedar was confused.

"I'm coming with you," her mother said.

"Really?" Cedar was happy. Then she remembered that the reason why she had to go north in the first place was because her mother needed someone to watch her while she went to work every day.

"What about your job?" she asked.

"Oh, everything is okay, I took some time off. I have a few weeks of vacation time coming to me. Your Great Auntie is getting older and I just got off the phone with your father. It looks like she could use some help around the house now."

She finished packing their snacks into a little cooler for their bus trip. "Besides, I miss hanging out with you when you're up there without me."Cedar crossed the kitchen and hugged her mother very tightly.

The next morning Cedar and her mother got on the bus. Cedar slept against the window while her mother read one of her romance books, the kind that had guys with long hair and no shirts on the front cover. When she woke up, Cedar ate her cucumber sandwiches and drank juice with her mom.

It was sunny and hot outside when they got off the bus.

"Dad!" Cedar yelled and ran to her father who was waiting in his usual spot at the bus depot.

"Hi, John," her mom said, hugging him.

"Good to see you, Mary." Cedar's mom and dad hadn't lived together since she was a baby, but they were still friends. Her mom said it was because they both loved her so much and they had that in common.

They drove across the bay to Auntie's house, singing country tunes at the top of their lungs. Dad helped them carry their suitcases up the porch and promised to be back for lunch the next day.

Auntie was sleeping so they crept in quietly, holding the screen door so it wouldn't swing back and make a loud bang. Mom started making tea in the kitchen while Cedar sat on the couch. Just as the kettle started to whistle, Auntie's bedroom door opened.

"Cedar! Mary!" She smiled and opened her arms. Mom hugged her first. Auntie looked really small then, like a little girl with curly grey hair. Then Cedar hugged her. She noticed how fragile her Great Auntie felt, like a little bird.

Cedar and her mom spent that summer cleaning her Auntie's house, cooking meals and tending to the yard work. Aunt Flora was a lot slower now, but only her body. Her mind was still quick as a fox and she could still beat anyone in cards. The whole extended family would come over on Saturdays to eat a meal together and chat. By nightfall, at least one fiddle or a couple of guitars would be pulled out and music would fill the little house, riding the breezes all the way down to the Georgian Bay so that even the turtles in the lake could dance a jig if they wanted.

Aunt Flora had fun that summer. She would clap her hands and tap her worn out moccasins on the floor. She was indeed happy to be with her whole family. Soon August was almost over and Cedar and her mother packed up their red and blue suitcases for the bus ride home. The night before they got on the bus, Auntie, Cedar and Mary sat at the kitchen table together. Auntie was showing Mary how to tack down a line of beads on a creamy piece of animal hide.

"You're such a good teacher, Aunt Flora," Mary said, marveling at how easily she had learned to bead the right way from the older woman.

Cedar piped up. "Yeah, mom. Auntie's taught me all kinds of cool things too."

Her mother smiled, "Really? Did you learn how to bead too?"

"No, I learned about Humility, Bravery, Respect, Truth, Wisdom and Honesty." She counted them off on her fingers.

Mom put the hide down, "Really? That's great! Those are really important things to know. They sound like the Seven Grandfathers to me."

Great Auntie looked up, "Yes, they are the Grandfathers."

Cedar wrinkled her forehead, "But there are only six? I'm still missing one."

Auntie chuckled. "No, my girl, you aren't missing anything. The last teaching is Love and you've reminded me about that one all by yourself this summer."

"How, Auntie?" Cedar asked curiously.

“Why, just by being here, my girl. By helping me with the dishes and playing real quiet when I’m sleeping and of course sharing your good mother with me all summer long. You already know all about Love.”

Cedar thought about all the old woman had shown her. “Auntie, you showed me that teaching every year. Every summer I came here you told me stories and let me go with you on walks and to pick medicine.”

Auntie’s eyes were filled with tears now. Her smile was so big it made her eyes crinkle up. Cedar smiled back. “I guess I’m a pretty lucky girl to have received these seven gifts. Chi Miigwetch.”

Cedar hugged her Auntie at the kitchen table. She hugged her so tight she could feel the old woman’s heartbeat in her own chest. Cedar was very grateful for all the gifts her Great Auntie had given her. They would last a life time. All her summers on Georgian Bay had made her feel like this was truly her home.

Word List:

Anishinaabe

Bravery

Chi Miigwetch

Confession

Depot

Honesty

Humility

Love

Pimaatisiwin

Respect

Truth

Wisdom

Unison

Grade 2 Sight Words

The Dolch words are the 220 most frequently found words in books that children read. These words are usually learned in first and second grade; students who learn these words have a good base for beginning reading. Many of these words cannot be sounded out because they do not follow the 'rules,' so they must be learned as sight words.

Pre-Primer Dolch Words (40 spelling words)

a	and	away	big	blue
can	come	down	find	for
funny	go	help	here	I
in	is	it	jump	little
look	make	me	my	not
one	play	red	run	said
see	the	three	to	two
up	we	where	yellow	you

Primer Dolch Words (52 spelling words)

all	am	are	at	ate
be	black	brown	but	came
did	do	eat	four	get
good	have	he	into	like
must	new	no	now	on
our	out	please	pretty	ran
ride	saw	say	she	so
soon	that	there	they	this
too	under	want	was	well
went	what	white	who	will
with	yes			

First Grade Dolch Words (41 spelling words)

after	again	an	any	as
ask	by	could	every	fly
from	give	going	had	has
her	him	his	how	just
know	let	live	may	of
old	once	open	over	put
round	some	stop	take	thank
them	then	think	walk	were
when				

Second Grade Dolch Words (46 spelling words)

always	around	because	been	before
best	both	buy	call	cold
does	don't	fast	first	five
found	gave	goes	green	its
made	many	off	or	pull
read	right	sing	sit	sleep
tell	their	these	those	upon
us	use	very	wash	which
why	wish	work	would	write
your				

Third Grade Dolch Words (41 spelling words)

about	better	bring	carry	clean
cut	done	draw	drink	eight
fall	far	full	got	grow
hold	hot	hurt	if	keep
kind	laugh	light	long	much
myself	never	only	own	pick
seven	shall	show	six	small
start	ten	today	together	try
warm				